THE STORY OF

RANDOM HOUSE · NEW YORK

Kíng Arthur

By **CLIFTON FADIMAN**

Illustrated by PAUL LIBEROVSKY

Merlin Foretells the Future

In olden times there lived in ancient England (which was then called Britain) a great king named Uther Pendragon. The island was ruled by many small lords called barons, each of whom lived in his castle and was master of all of his land. These fierce barons fought among themselves; but they all obeyed and served the King of Britain, the great Uther Pendragon.

The king's closest friends and advisers were a brave knight called Ulfius and a powerful magician named Merlin. Merlin had a long white beard and a wrinkled old wise face. With his magic he could do strange and wonderful things. He was also good and kind, using his powers for the benefit of Britain and its king.

After ruling his kingdom for a number of years, Uther took to wife the gentle and beautiful lady Igraine. After a while they had a boy whom they named Arthur. He was a strong and lovely baby with golden hair and blue eyes. King Uther was very proud of him.

One day the magician Merlin, his face thoughtful, approached the king.

After Uther had invited him to seat himself, the magician said, "As you know, my powers allow me to foretell the future. Looking into my magic crystal, I saw that you will shortly fall ill of a fever and perhaps die. Therefore I think it wise for you to protect your newborn son Arthur. For if you die, he will be in danger. The warring barons, knowing him to be the only rightful King of England, will try as hard as they can to see that he never succeeds to the throne."

The king was much disturbed by his wise magician's prophecy. He did not fear death, but he was upset by Merlin's warning about his son. Were Uther to die, the baby would be in danger of his life. The king sat and thought for a few minutes, Merlin standing silent before him. Finally he spoke:

"You have never advised me, Merlin, unless you had a plan. What is it?"

"Permit Lord Ulfius and myself to convey Arthur to a secret place known only to us where, were you to die, he will be safe and can grow to manhood. Then later he will be able to claim his rights. England will have need of Arthur who, I foretell, will be the greatest king the world has ever known."

Instantly King Uther made up his mind. As fearless and honorable as he was old and wise, he thought to himself that if his death were fated, there was nothing he could do about *that*. But he could make sure that Arthur would live to become the next king. Uther nodded his head.

Late that night, Merlin and Lord Ulfius, disguised in dark cloaks, crept to the nursery. The castle was in darkness, lit only by the rush torches flickering in the draught that whipped and wailed through the dank stone corridors. The old nurse had been called away by the king on some pretext, and for five minutes the baby was alone. He was sleeping in his silver cradle, the arms of Uther Pendragon embroidered in silk above

his little head. Quietly Merlin picked up the baby, cradle and all, and he and Ulfius crept down the stairs and out of the castle.

And none but these two, Merlin and Ulfius, knew to what place Arthur had been taken.

Chapter Two

The Death of Uther Pendragon

Shortly afterward King Uther, as Merlin had foretold, fell ill and died. The realm of Britain was left without a king, and the barons and lords began to quarrel over who should take Uther's place. Instead of being loyal to one man and one ruler, they were now loyal only to themselves. They took poor peasants and forced them into their private armies. All over Britain countless small and bloody wars broke out. Neighbor fought neighbor. With everyone busy fighting there was no time to sow and harvest crops, and famine gripped the land. In the time of King Uther travelers upon the broad highway had been safe. Now the cruel barons turned bandit and harried the highways as they pleased. They took innocent travelers prisoner. If the captives were rich, they held them for ransom. If not, they made slaves of them or killed them.

This wild and dreadful time lasted for eighteen years, during which Arthur was growing to young manhood. Only two men knew where the rightful King of Britain was hidden. And they told no one.

One day the Archbishop of Canterbury sent for Merlin. The great magician arrived as fast as he could. Eighteen years had passed, leaving him unchanged. His beard was still snowy white, his black eyes sparkled beneath his frowning forehead. He bowed to the Archbishop and waited in silence.

"Merlin," the Archbishop said, "men tell me that you are the wisest man in England. We have been leaderless now for eighteen years and Britain is drowned in blood. Can you think of a way to stop this lawlessness?

Find us a king, Merlin. Only a strong and wise leader can defend us against our enemies and give us happiness again."

Merlin stood silent for a moment. Then he lifted his eyes to the face of the old Archbishop.

"My lord, as you know, I can sometimes foretell the future. I foretold the unhappy illness that struck down King Uther. Now I can tell you that Britain is soon to have a

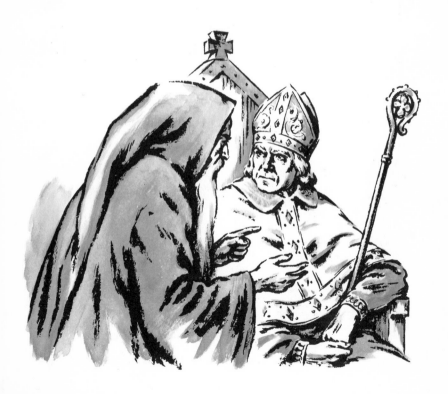

king who will be even wiser, greater, nobler than Uther Pendragon. He will bring order and peace where now there is disorder and war. The whole world will talk of him and his name will go down in history on the lips of men."

The Archbishop moved uneasily on his great thronelike chair.

"All very well, Merlin. But the country will find it difficult to accept such a king coming from God knows where, born out of darkness and mystery. What blood will this lord carry in his veins? Will he be royal and hold Britain first in his heart? These are serious questions demanding careful answers."

Merlin's seamed face broke into a reassuring smile.

"I promise you that this king will be of Uther Pendragon's own royal blood."

"How can you foretell this?" the old Archbishop asked. He made a motion with his hands. "No, I will trust you, Merlin. You have always worked for what is good, and your powers have ever been at the service of your country and your king. But answer me this. There are many lesser kings who feel themselves worthy to lead Britain. How then shall we know the real king from the others?"

"My lord Archbishop," Merlin said, "with your leave I shall use my magic to create a test of kingship. He who passes this test shall thus show all the world that he is the rightful overlord of this country."

And with this the Archbishop was content.

Chapter Three

The Sword
in the Anvil

By his magic Merlin caused a huge white marble stone to appear in an open place before the gates of the greatest church in London. Upon this block of marble there stood an iron anvil. Thrust into the anvil almost to its hilt was a naked sword. The hilt was embroidered with gold and inlaid with precious stones. The blade was of blue steel and where the sun struck it dazzled the eyes. Upon the stone in letters of gold were inlaid these words:

WHOSO DRAWETH OUT THIS SWORD FROM

THE ANVIL IS THE RIGHTFUL

KING OF BRITAIN

There was a brightness and a glory about the sword that had never been seen before. Even in the night it shone with a light of its own, shedding a soft golden radiance. News spread far and wide of the great magical sword in the anvil. Those who dared approach it closely noticed that the iron of the anvil seemed part of the steel blade and the steel blade part of the iron. When they read the magic golden words written upon the stone the people murmured among themselves, for it seemed impossible that any man could pull the sword from the anvil.

Now as Christmas week approached, the Archbishop called together all the nobles, that each might try his hand at drawing the sword. The one who could do so would become King of England.

Soon it seemed as though the entire world

was wending its way to London. The highways were filled with people—kings and lords and knights and ladies and pages and men-at-arms. All were traveling to London, where there was to be the greatest tournament ever held, and where all men of noble birth were invited at the end of the tournament to try to pull out the sword. Every inn and rooming house was full to overflowing. Everywhere along the road were ranged tents and pavilions pitched for the accommodation of those who could not find shelter within doors.

When the Archbishop saw the incredible multitude who had come to London for the adventure, he turned to Merlin and said hopefully, "Surely among so many nobles and lords we shall find someone worthy of being King of England."

Merlin smiled. "Marvel not if among all these there appears not one worthy. And also marvel not if among those who are unknown there rises up one who shall prove himself entirely worthy. For out of the mud and the earth bloom the most beautiful flowers."

The Archbishop grew silent, pondering the words of the great magician.

Chapter Four

The Great Tournament at London

Among the noblemen who journeyed to London town to try their luck in the tournament and at the adventure of the Sword in the Stone was a middle-aged knight, highly born, named Sir Ector of Bonnemaison. His fame was great. Never had he been known to break his word to peasant or prince, never had he betrayed a confidence. He was rich besides, with many castles in Wales—rich not only in money, but also in his wife and his two sons. The elder, a young knight of great courage and reputation, was called Sir Kay. The younger son, only eighteen, was still a page. His name was Arthur.

When Sir Ector had first received the summons of the Archbishop he called his sons to him. "We are going to London," he said. The two young men were filled with excitement, for they lived a quiet life in the country and had never been to any large town before, much less London, the greatest town on earth.

Then there was a hustling and a bustling in the castle. All great lords like Sir Ector lived surrounded by manservants, who did the everyday work of the castle in return for food and keep. These retainers, squires and pages had all to make themselves ready for the journey. The castle had to be cleaned inside and out. This they did by strewing great bundles of rushes on the stone floor, covering up the dirt of the previous year. It was a common joke that one could tell what one's grandfather had eaten for supper, fifty years before, just by digging down into the layers of rushes until the fiftieth one was reached.

Sir Ector's armor and Kay's too were polished again and again by the old armorer. Then the armor was coated with bear grease to make it even more slippery, so that the spear-points of the opposing knights would glance off.

When Kay saw all these preparations he was filled with great hope.

"Sir," he said, "is it possible that you will let me enter the tournament?"

Kay spoke casually, but he did not fool Sir Ector, who saw the blood rushing to his cheeks.

The old lord smiled. "Yes," he said, "if you wish to." It was clear that Kay wished to, for he clapped his hands together and gave a loud cheer. Then he colored to his fiery hair, for though he was trying hard to be dignified, he had shown his emotions like a small boy.

But Sir Ector understood. It would be Kay's first grown-up tournament, a tournament which would probably be the most exciting England had seen in fifty years.

So Kay sent in his credentials to the congress of heralds. After considering his claims they admitted his name to the list of knights permitted to fight in the tourney. In all the length and breadth of England there was no happier young man than Sir Kay.

After four days' journey Sir Ector, Kay, Arthur and the retinue of servants and men-

at-arms reached the town of London. They set up camp in a broad field near the place where the tournament was to be held. Sir Ector's pavilion was of green silk, the arms of his house embroidered upon it.

There were numberless other pavilions pitched in the meadow. The grass, newly cut for this occasion, gleamed green. The flags and pennons and embroidered coats-of-arms fluttered in the English breeze—gold and red and blue—almost covering the green meadow and partly shutting out the blue sky above.

There were young men everywhere, sitting in the sun, proudly polishing their helmets. Some of the older ones had already fastened a wispy silk handkerchief or a lock of hair to their helmets, to show that they had a lady-love who wished them success in the tournament.

Kay wandered about the meadow. A group of young knights of his own age were practicing tilting at the quintain. The quintain was a battered post painted in blue and red. The young men charged it, trying to hook an iron ring with their spears. The man who hooked the most rings was declared the winner.

Kay, who loved horses, never grew tired of seeing the black and white and dappled war steeds lumbering toward the iron post. Each knight, his greased armor flashing in the light of the sun, crouched low over his horse's neck, his great ash-wood spear held out stiffly before him. The iron-plated spear butt was nestled under one armpit, and a gauntleted hand grasped the spear at the point where it had been thinned down for a hand-hold.

The gay feathers attached to the visors of the helmets nodded in the breeze. The sun shone down on all. Kay felt a wonderful lightness in his heart, a feeling that something good was about to happen to him.

And Arthur? Arthur's waiting time was quite different. As Kay's page he had a lot of work to do. First there was the armor to polish and repolish, and then there was the messy business of smearing grease on the armor. There was the sharpening of Kay's sword and spear-point. This spear-point, made of iron, was sharpened by hand on a piece of sandstone. It was a tricky business; Arthur had to hold the spear-point at just the right angle so as not to nick the sharp edges. It took him quite a while, for the point had been battered by some of Kay's misses at the quintain, but he finally managed it.

If Kay was unkind to his younger brother Arthur, it was not that he meant to be. It was only that Arthur was his page. It was the custom to treat pages as though they were unimportant, which they were, though when they grew up they would become knights, and then *they* would treat *their* pages as unimportant too.

Toward afternoon Arthur was through with his chores and could rest. He didn't quite know what to do with himself. Finally he turned his steps toward London. After all, he had never seen it.

London was a town of tiny crooked ways, littered with garbage and liquid mud. The smells were dreadful. Arthur had to dodge the refuse that was occasionally thrown from the windows of the two-story wooden houses that lined the lanes. Yet it was all strange and wonderful.

As young Arthur turned a sharp corner he saw the most wonderful thing of all. The great church with its stone goblins frowning down (they were supposed to ward off evil) stood foursquare in the heart of London town. Arthur approached it with reverence and delight.

It was then that he noticed the sword in the anvil. He looked at it idly, not even reading the inscription, thinking to himself, So that's what all the talk is about! And he turned away.

As Arthur was a young page, not yet admitted to the councils of men, his knowledge of the miraculous sword was incomplete. He knew it had something to do with the King of England, but that was all. The older knights did not allow him to listen to them when they discussed the great adventure appointed for Christmas day.

Arthur turned homeward. It did not occur to him to wonder why the weather was so beautiful at this time of the year. With not a hint of snow in the air, it was almost as warm as spring. Even the grass in the great meadow was still summer grass.

The day of the tournament dawned bright and sunny. A huge throng was gathered to witness the great show. Tournaments were serious business for this was the way that young men trained for war and feats of arms. No fewer than twenty thousand lords and ladies (besides twelve foreign kings and seven dukes) were on hand to watch.

In the center of all the noise and splendor rose the throne of the Archbishop himself. It was hung with velvet embroidered with the figure of St. George in gold. A canopy of purple cloth embroidered with silver lilies was draped above the throne. Upon this gorgeous seat sat the Archbishop surrounded by his court. His throne seemed the heart of a many-colored splendid flower, for the other great lords and ladies of the land had brought with them their own canopies and thrones. Theirs were smaller, of course, the Archbishop being the most powerful of them all.

When everyone was in his place a herald in crimson and gold stood before the throne of the Archbishop and blew a long loud blast upon his trumpet. At the signal two parties of knights entered the meadow—one from the north, the other from the south. The field was filled with the glitter and movement of their

horses. Lances bristled to the sky. The two groups took up their positions.

Sir Kay and his companions were at the north end of the field. Ninety-three knights made up his company, while the opposing side had ninety-six. However, Sir Kay's party, while fewer than the other by three men, boasted some of the best knights in the world.

When the two companies were ready, the herald put his trumpet to his lips and blew a second call. After a few minutes' wait he blew a third call, loud and long.

When the last notes had died away the knights spurred their horses and rushed forth in headlong combat. As the two knightly companies met in the middle of the field the earth shook beneath the pounding of almost two hundred horses.

So terrible was the noise of breaking lances that several ladies fainted in fright. The air was dark with bits of iron and the dust raised made it almost impossible to see what was happening.

In this first onset forty knights were overthrown, many trampled beneath the hoofs of their horses. After the companies had withdrawn to their stations at the north and south of the meadow, the ground was seen to be covered with fragments of lances and pieces of armor. In the middle of the wreckage lay many knights dazed and unconscious. Some were able to rise; others could not and lay quietly as if dead. To these ran many pages and men-at-arms to lift and bear the fallen champions to their own pavilions and tents. Other attendants gathered up the pieces of ashwood and armor that littered the ground. Soon the battlefield was once more clear.

The watching assembly gave a long cheer. Never before in the history of England had there been so great a tournament.

From his elder brother's pavilion Arthur watched, praying, "Please, please, dear God, make me a knight soon." His blood ran hot through his veins and he could hardly stop himself from snatching up a short-sword and joining Sir Kay out on the field.

As for Kay, he bore himself with much heroism. On the assault no man of his company did better than he. Two knights had rushed down upon him, but he had unhorsed them. One he hit so violently with the side of his lance that he lifted him from the saddle and hurled him to the ground. Over and over in the dust rolled the knight.

Now the second part of the contest was beginning. Each knight handed his spear to his page (Arthur received Kay's spear) and drew his short-sword. The second assault was to be made with short-swords only.

Once more the herald blew his trumpet. Every one of the hundred-and-fifty-odd remaining champions drew his flashing blade. As the herald blew a second time the two companies rode one upon the other with great violence.

The blood of the knights ran hot and fierce now. Sir Kay seemed unbeatable, unhorsing five opponents before being stopped. A certain knight named Sir Balamorgineas, a huge man head and shoulders above all others, noted Kay especially. Famous for his enormous strength, Balamorgineas boasted that he could withstand the assault of three ordinary men at once.

In a bellow audible even above the din of the tourney he cried, "Ho Ho! Sir knight of the black armor, turn and do battle with me!"

Now when Sir Kay heard these words he spurred his horse, shouting, in a voice as loud as his opponent's, his acceptance of the challenge. Riding down upon Sir Balamorgineas, he hit at him with all his might. The big knight received the stroke of the sword full upon his helmet, the violence of the blow dizzying him. He had to hold onto his saddle to keep from falling off his horse.

Unfortunately Sir Kay's marvelous blow was so fierce that it broke his own sword off short. The young knight was left weaponless.

When Sir Balamorgineas saw this he fell furiously upon Kay. It would have gone badly for the young knight if he had not been as-

sisted by three of his friends. Seeing his terrible plight they rode down upon the huge knight and so Sir Kay was able to save himself with honor, for he was not required to fight until he had a sword once more in his hand.

As Kay reached his pavilion Arthur came running to him with a goblet of wine in his hand. Sir Kay threw back the visor of his helmet. His face streamed with blood and sweat. He tried to speak but could only croak hoarsely. He took the wine and drank it down. Then, his throat loosened, he said to Arthur, "Brother! Get me another sword to do battle, for I am winning much glory for our house this day!"

"Where shall I get you a sword?"

"Go to our father's pavilion and fetch me another sword with all speed, brother."

Arthur nodded his head and set off running. He had to be back before the battle was over or people would think that Kay had stayed away out of cowardice.

At the pavilion Arthur looked everywhere, but there was no spare sword. Nor did he find any servant, squire or man-at-arms from whom he could borrow one. He sat down for a moment in despair. He must bring a sword to his brother without delay.

Then he recalled the sword in the stone he had seen the day before. Anxious to get his brother a weapon and with no other thought in his head, he ran with all speed to the church. It was deserted, for everyone was at the tournament. The marble stone was there, the shining sword sticking out of the anvil. The place stood peaceful under the golden sun.

Without thinking Arthur leaped upon the marble stone and put his hand to the hilt of the sword. It fitted his fingers as though made for them. He bent his body and pulled strongly. Smoothly and easily out of the anvil came the sword.

He wrapped it in his cloak to hide its glitter. Leaping down from the marble stone, he ran back to the tournament.

He took the sword from his cloak and, panting, handed it to his brother. When Kay saw the sword he turned white, for he knew what it was and what it meant. For a moment he stood staring at it, as though turned to stone. Then he said in a strange voice, "Where did you get this sword?"

Arthur wondered why Kay's face was bloodless, his lips tight and strained.

"What is the matter, brother? I have nothing to hide. I found no sword in our father's pavilion, so I thought of the one fixed in the anvil upon the marble stone before the cathedral. I ran there and tried to draw it out of the anvil and it came out with ease. So I wrapped it in my cloak, that thieves might not see it gleaming, and brought it to you that you might do honor to our house upon the field of battle."

Then, holding the sword in his lap, Sir Kay sat down upon the ground and began to think. "My young brother," he said to himself, "is hardly more than a child. He does not know what he has done, or what it means to have done it. Since he has managed to draw this sword, why can I not say that I drew it forth, and take the glory for myself? After all, Arthur is only a boy, and I am a knight with a great reputation."

He looked up and spoke sternly to his younger brother. "Tell no one of what you have done. Meanwhile go to our father and tell him to come to me directly."

Arthur swallowed his questions and did as Kay told him. He could not understand why his brother appeared so disturbed. When Sir Ector heard the message he excused himself and set out in all haste toward his pavilion, fearing that Sir Kay had been wounded.

Chapter Five

Arthur Discovers the Secret of His Birth

At the pavilion they saw Sir Kay standing there, his face white as paper, his eyes shining. Sir Ector went up to him and put his hand on his shoulder.

"My son, what is the matter?"

"A wonderful thing has happened." Sir Kay took his father by the hand and led him to a table. Upon it lay a black cloak with something under it. Sir Kay opened the cloak. There lay the sword, its hilt and blade glistening in the sunlight.

Recognizing it immediately, Sir Ector was so astonished that for a minute he could not speak. Then he cried out, "What is this that my eyes behold?"

"Sire," Kay said, "I have that sword which stood a while since embedded in the anvil that stands upon the marble stone before the great cathedral. I would ask you as my father what this means."

"Kay," Sir Ector said softly, "how did you get this sword?"

For a moment Kay was silent. Then he said slowly, "Father, I broke my own sword in battle and I found this one in its stead."

Arthur was sorely tempted to speak out; but, taught respect for his elders, he remained silent.

Sir Ector did not know whether to believe Kay or not. After a while he put his arm around his elder son.

"Kay," he said, "if you did draw forth this sword from the anvil then it must also be that you are the rightful King of England, for so

the writing around the base of the anvil pro-
claims. But if you have truly drawn it out of
the anvil, then it should be easy for you to
thrust it back again."

Then Kay, guilty and troubled, said furiously, "Who can do such a thing as thrust a
sword into solid iron? It would take a miracle
to do that."

"Such a miracle is no greater than that of
taking it out of the iron," Sir Ector said slowly.

"Whoever heard of a man that could draw forth a sword from a place and yet could not thrust it back from whence he drew it?"

Kay decided to brazen it out. If Arthur, his younger brother, was able to perform this miracle, why could he not do the same? For was he not a full-fledged knight and Arthur but a boy?

He wrapped the sword in the cloak and he and Sir Ector made their way to the marble stone in front of the cathedral. Arthur went along with them, keeping in the background, and his brother and father said nothing to him. When they reached the cathedral, Sir Kay mounted the marble stone and looked at the iron face of the anvil. It was smooth and polished, with not a crack or scratch to show that a sword had once been embedded in the iron block.

Then in his heart Kay knew that he could never perform the miracle. But he had to go through with it. Putting the sword-point to the anvil, with all his weight he bore down upon the iron. Nothing happened.

After he had tried until he was red in the face and gasping for breath, he leaped down from the stone and said to his father, angrily, "Father, no man can perform such a miracle."

"Then how was it possible for you to draw the sword from solid iron?"

At this point young Arthur lifted up his head. "Father, have I leave to speak?" Sir Ector nodded. Arthur said, "Could I try?"

"Son," Sir Ector said, "this is a sacred matter, not for striplings. By what authority do you dare handle the sword?"

"Because it was I who drew it from the anvil for my brother's sake," Arthur replied. "And since I drew it out it should not be too hard to put it back."

Then Sir Ector looked at Arthur with a strange wild look, and Arthur cried out, "Father, why do you look upon me so? Have I angered you?"

"No, my son. I am not angry. If you wish to try your hand with the sword, do so."

Arthur took the sword from his brother Kay. He leaped up upon the marble stone. He put the point to the smooth iron and bore down strongly upon it. And behold! The sword slipped smoothly into the center of the anvil

35

and stood there half-embedded in the solid metal.

Not content with this, he drew the sword out of the anvil and put it back once more.

When Sir Ector beheld what his younger son had done, he cried out, "Lord, Lord!" in a loud voice. And as Arthur descended from the marble stone Sir Ector kneeled before him and put his hands together palm to palm.

Seeing his old father thus, Arthur cried out in anguish, "My father! Why do you kneel before me?"

"Well do I know that I am not your father," Sir Ector said, still kneeling, "and the blood you come from is nobler than mine or than any in the land."

Then Arthur began to cry and said through his tears, "Father, do not kneel before me. I beg you to rise for I do not understand your words."

So Sir Ector rose from his knees and stood before Arthur and said gently, "Why do you weep, Arthur?"

And Arthur said, "Because I am sore afraid."

All this while Sir Kay had stood near by,

neither speaking nor moving but thinking to himself, "Why, what is this? My brother a king?"

Then Sir Ector said, "Arthur, the time has come for you to know who you are, for the true story of your life has been hidden from

you and from the world. Listen to my words.

"Eighteen years ago there came to me a certain man, wise and much in favor with King Uther Pendragon. He was the enchanter Merlin. Showing me the ring of Uther Pendragon, Merlin commanded me in the king's name to be at a lonely place, alone, at a particular time. The place was to be the back gate of Uther Pendragon's castle and the time midnight of that very day.

"Warning me upon pain of death to tell no man of this adventure, he departed. At midnight of that day I stood outside the back gate of the castle as I had been told to do, and there came to me Merlin and another, a great knight named Sir Ulfius; and Merlin had in his arms a bundle wrapped in red linen. When he opened the folds of the mantle I beheld a baby, newborn, still wrapped in swaddling clothes. He was a beautiful child," Sir Ector said, his voice gentle at the memory, "well-made, with a fair face. And you, Arthur, were that child.

"Then Merlin commanded me to take the child and rear it as my own. He said that its name was to be Arthur, and no one in the world was to know it was not mine. I gave Merlin my promise, took the child, and returned home. My dear wife raised it as her own, and except for her no one in the world ever knew that you were not my true son."

The old man paused, gathering his thoughts. Then he went on, "I never asked who your father was, Arthur, nor did Merlin tell me. But now I suspect that he was the great Uther Pendragon himself, for who but his son could have drawn the sword from the anvil?" And the old man fell silent, looking upon Arthur with love and awe.

Then Arthur cried out in a loud voice, "Woe!" His eyes filled again with tears.

"Why are you sad?" Sir Ector asked him.

"Because I have lost my father," Arthur said, "and I would rather have my father than be king!"

At this point there came into the church-yard two men of noble appearance. They were none other than Merlin and Sir Ulfius. As they approached, Merlin said in a deep voice, "What cheer?"

"Cheer of a wonderful sort," Sir Ector said, "for here is the boy that you brought me by night and in secrecy eighteen years ago, and he has grown to manhood."

'Then Sir Ulfius smiled and Merlin raised his hands. A deep hush fell over the small group. Merlin began to speak.

"Sir Ector, I know who this boy is, for I have kept watch over him all these years. I know that in him there lies the hope of Britain. Moreover I tell you that today in my magic crystal I saw how twice he drew the sword forth from the anvil and thrust it back again. What you have told him, good Sir Ector, is nothing but the truth. And I prophesy that Arthur will become the greatest and most famous king who ever lived in Britain; and I foresee that many knights of valor and bravery will gather about him and men will tell of their glorious deeds. Arthur, your reign will be one of splendor and you will have marvelous adventures. The most marvelous adventure of them all, that of the Holy Grail, will be achieved by three of the knights of your court. Sir Ector, keep this young man safe and sound, for in him lies the hope and the salvation of all this realm of Britain."

Then Sir Ector lifted his voice and asked a

boon of Arthur. Arthur's eyes filled with tears. He nodded his head only, and Sir Ector said, "When you are king, my lord, grant me this wish: that your brother Kay be guardian and protector of all this realm under you."

Arthur nodded his head again and said, "So shall it be." He raised up Sir Ector and said to him, "Sir, you will always be my father." And then he sat down upon the ground and began to weep. And no man could stop his tears.

Chapter Six

How Young Arthur Became King Arthur

On Christmas day the Archbishop gathered together all the kings and nobles to try the adventure of the sword, and a great number of gentlefolk and simple people collected in front of the cathedral to watch.

After the Archbishop had seated himself, the herald blew his trumpet, and the kings began to come forward. One after the other tried to draw the sword from the anvil and failed. Some grew red in the face and angry, some were much downcast, but it availed them nothing. After them came seven dukes, but they too were unable to perform the miracle. Then the high lords and nobles of the land put their hands to the miraculous sword. It budged not one inch.

The Archbishop's advisors then spoke to him. "No man can achieve this adventure," they told him. "All that is happening is that you are being made foolish. The best in the land have tried to draw the sword from the iron, and none has succeeded. It would be wiser to stop this mockery now, and to choose from these highborn princes the future King of Britain."

While the Archbishop was pondering these matters, Merlin went to the pavilion of Sir Ector and said to Arthur, "Arise and come forth, for now the hour is come for you to try before the world that miracle which you have already accomplished in private."

So Arthur arose and proceeded to the cathedral with his father and Sir Kay and Merlin, walking as if in a dream.

He was clad that day in flame-colored clothes embroidered with silver threads. As he passed the people looked long at him, wondering who he was. Merlin and Arthur paused in front of the Archbishop, and the old man looked down from his great throne, saying, "Who are these, Merlin, and what is their business here?"

"Here is one who has come to try the adventure of the sword," Merlin said, pointing to Arthur.

The Archbishop asked: "By what right does he come here?"

"By the best right in the world," Merlin answered, "for this young man in flame-colored clothes is the true son of Uther Pendragon and his lawful wife Queen Igraine."

Then the Archbishop cried out in amazement, and smiled upon Arthur and bade him try his hand at the sword. So Arthur strode to the great stone and stood upon its lip. Taking the pommel of the sword in his hand, he pulled, and it came smoothly out. He swung

the sword over his head, and the gleam of its blade was like lightning. After he had swung it about he slipped the sword back into the anvil smoothly and easily. Then, as the huge crowd roared its approval and acclaim, Arthur drew out the sword and put it back again three times before all the people. And after that some of the kings and nobles retired to their homes in indignation that a beardless boy should become king. But others pressed forward and laid their swords at Arthur's feet.

Some days later he was crowned and

anointed and became rightful king of all Britain. He made Kay seneschal of his lands and advanced his foster father to a high place in the court. So he kept his word to his family. Then he began to look about him for a wife, for it was not fitting that a king should reign without a queen.

Chapter Seven

Arthur's Wedding and the Round Table

For two years Arthur sought a queen to share his throne. During that time he was busy fighting two wars and uniting his kingdom. The great barons and lords who had not acknowledged him rightful King of Britain were brought to their knees. Before twenty-four months had passed Britain was again a realm for all men. Food was harvested and law prevailed over all the kingdom.

To enforce these laws Arthur drew about him a glorious company of knights who went forth as special representatives of Arthur's court to make sure that his commands were obeyed.

Arthur searched far and wide for a queen, finding her at last at the court of King Leodegrance, one of his most faithful lords. This king had a beautiful daughter named Guinevere with whom Arthur fell in love, even serving for two weeks as her gardener's boy. When he revealed himself to Leodegrance and asked for Guinevere's hand, he had already won the lady's heart, even in disguise. So they plighted their troth.

In the fall of the year Arthur and Guinevere were wed. The place of their wedding was Arthur's favorite castle, Camelot, and it was burnished bright for the occasion.

On his wedding morning Arthur sat in state in his royal hall, waiting for news of the royal bride. About the middle of the morning a messenger upon a milk-white steed came riding into the court. He was the herald of Guinevere's coming. Joyfully the king arose and went forth surrounded by his court to greet his lady. He brought her back in full splendor, arrayed as she was in cloth of gold; and for years afterward people talked of her beauty and Arthur's nobility.

At high noon the Archbishop married them and the Camelot bells rang out in joyous clangor. The court sat itself down to the wedding feast, and no man before had ever seen such food or such array. For the vessels were of solid gold, and you could not count the rich dishes passed by pages dressed in splendid livery.

But the most marvelous thing of all was Merlin's wedding gift to the royal couple. By his magic the enchanter caused a wondrously rich pavilion to be erected and in the center of it he created the Round Table. This table was in the shape of a great ring. There were exactly fifty places set upon it with fifty chairs and fifty gold glasses filled with magic wine. Merlin took Guinevere and Arthur by the hand and led them to the Round Table. They stopped short unable to speak.

"Merlin, what I see is wonderful beyond telling," said the king.

Merlin smiled, well pleased, and pointed

out to his king the marvelous virtues of the magic Round Table. First he showed him a seat set high above the others, wrought with precious woods and gilded with gold.

"Behold," he said, "this is the royal seat, and it is yours to sit in." As the magician spoke, there appeared letters of gold on the back of that seat:

KING ARTHUR

"This is the center seat of the Round Table," Merlin said. "For in truth, Arthur, you are the center of all that is most worthy of honor." Then the magician pointed to the seat that stood opposite the royal seat, and it too was of strange and marvelous appearance. "My lord," Merlin said, "that seat is called the Seat Perilous, for no man but one in all the world shall sit upon it, and that man is not yet born upon the earth. And if any other man dare sit there, he does so at mortal peril. Therefore is it called the Seat Perilous."

"This is most wonderful, Merlin," Arthur said, "but how am I to find the knights to put at this table? Do you find them for me, and right quickly."

Merlin smiled at the king. "Lord, why such haste? For when the Round Table is entirely filled then your glory will be entirely achieved and you will begin to decline. When a man's work is done, God breaks the man as a man might break a goblet from which such perfect wine has been drunk that no baser wine may follow after. So when your work is done, God will shatter the chalice of your life."

But Arthur looked steadfastly into Merlin's face and said, "Old man, you speak truly. Nevertheless I am in God's hands, and I would wish for His glory and His good to be done even though He shall then entirely break me when I have served His purposes."

"Spoken like a true king," Merlin said. "I cannot fill your table yet, but can find only two-and-thirty knights worthy of the Company of the Round Table."

"Then choose them quickly," said Arthur.

And Merlin said, "It shall be done."

So Merlin chose the two-and-thirty, and as he chose them in solemn assembly the name of each knight appeared by magic upon the back of his own seat, blazing in letters of gold. As each knight was chosen he took his place

at the Round Table. When they were all chosen, and all sitting there, Arthur sat down upon the royal seat. He called for the Archbishop, and the old man came in state. He blessed each of the seats, progressing from place to place, surrounded by his bishops. And after the blessing each knight rose in his

place and presented the hilt of his sword as a cross upon which to swear a mighty and holy oath. All assembled, they swore that they would be gentle to the weak, courageous before the strong; that they would be terrible to the wicked and the evildoer; that they would defend the helpless who should call upon them for aid; that they would hold all women as sacred; that they would help each other at all times, one man's enemy being the enemy of all; that they would be merciful to all men; and lastly, that they would be gentle in deed, pure in friendship, faithful in love. This was their mighty oath, the greatest ever sworn, and they swore it upon the hilt of their swords and kissed the hilts in witness of their swearing.

Then the whole company sat down at the Round Table and drank from the golden glasses and ate from the golden plates.

Arthur, sitting in the royal seat, found his eyes wandering to the Seat Perilous and wondered mightily who this very perfect knight would be. He was not to know it for many years, but the knight's name was to be Galahad, son of Sir Lancelot.

And so the young Arthur began his famous reign. In the days to come, he and his knights of the Round Table were to have many thrilling and wonderful adventures. But Arthur would never forget what had started it all—the miracle of the Sword, the Stone and the Anvil.

Legacy Books